Mimi Gets a TOOTH FILLING

Written By
Latia Smith, RDH

Illustrated By
Sameer Kassar

LUMINARE PRESS
WWW.LUMINAREPRESS.COM

Cover Design by Sameer Kassar

Luminare Press
442 Charnelton St.
Eugene, OR 97401
www.luminarepress.com

LCCN: 2023914309
ISBN: 979-8-88679-354-3

Dedicated to Tamisha "Mimi" Walden

People came from here and there

to gather for the county fair.

A pirate ship swayed side to side

as kids looped around on a Ferris wheel ride.

High in the air were flying swings that flew

above the farm animals in the petting zoo.

Children of all ages played games that were fun

like hitting a target with water from a gun.

Others shot basketballs into a net

and tried to make a hole-in-one during their set.

Mimi rode on a horse up and down

while Mama and Baby-sis sat on the side of the
merry-go-round.

The wind bought in a refreshing breeze

that smelled like delicious concession stand treats.

Famous hot dogs and funnel cakes

suddenly gave everyone a desire to taste.

They got in line, and there they stood

to try the food that smelled so good.

"Now you can pick out one sweet treat,"

Mama said to Mimi as she took a peek.

Cotton candy, ice cream cones,

fried cookies, and flavored snow cones.

Mimi's eyes glanced from side to side.

There were too many choices, but she had to decide.

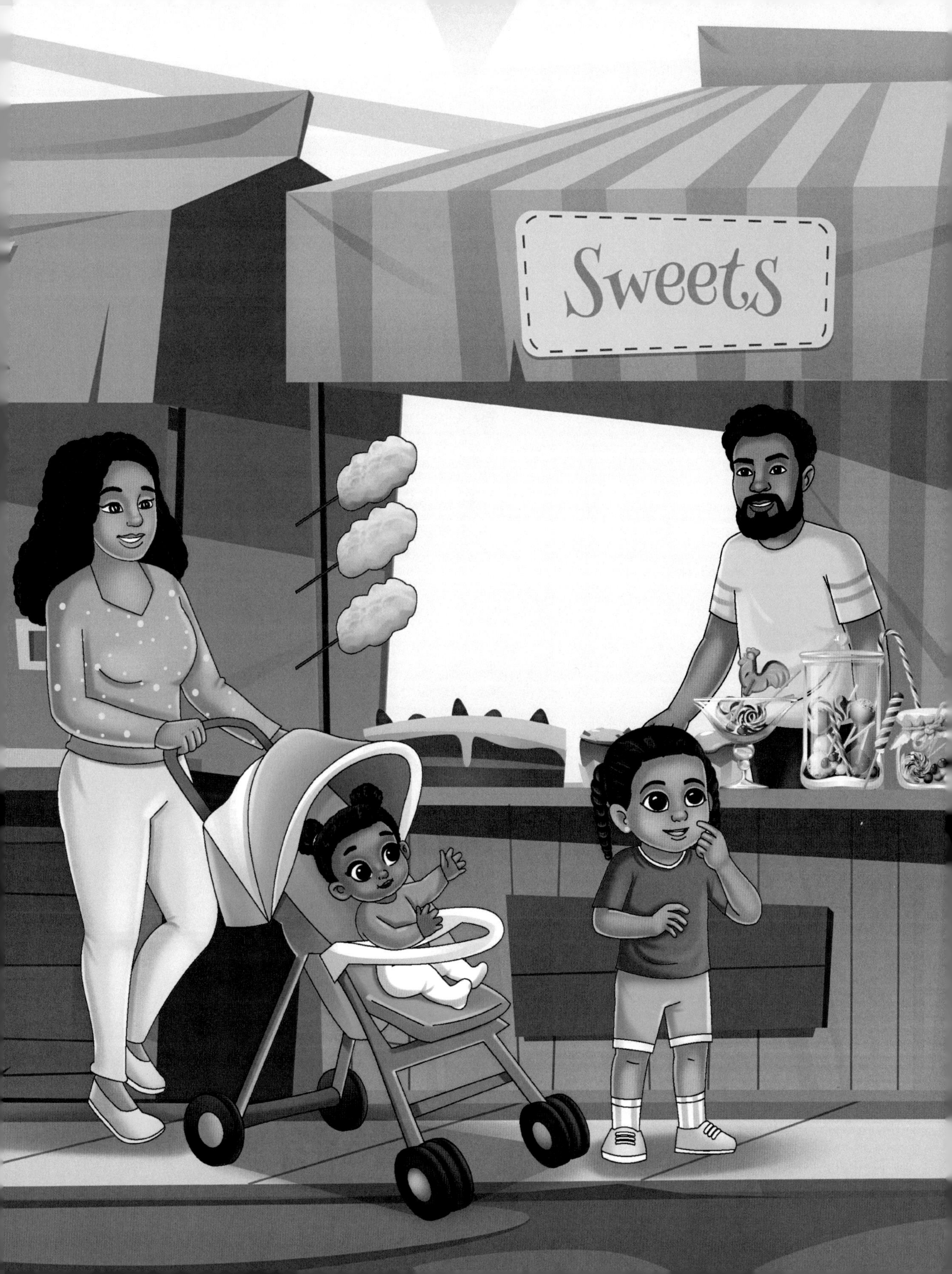
Sweets

A man behind the concession stand

placed something sweet in Mimi's hand.

A shiny gold candy apple

was tied with a bow in a see-through wrapper.

Then Mama asked, "What do you say?"

Mimi smiled and said, "Thank you! You made my day!"

While Mimi was having so much fun,

it was now time to entertain the little one.

They ventured off to an exciting place

where a make-up artist would paint their face.

With glitter, paint, and a beautiful design,

Baby-sis had a sparkly face that really shined!

A couple of swirls with colors so bright

came together for a look that Mimi thought was
just right.

Baby-sis' cheeks were covered and her nose was too.

Only her eyes could be seen for a game of peek-a-boo.

But when Mama looked at Mimi, she noticed a pout.

"What's wrong?" Mama asked. "What's that face about?"

"What seems to be troubling Mama's honey bun?"

Mimi didn't look like she was having any fun.

She handed Mama her apple; she had taken a bite.

But Mama was confused. "Are you alright?"

Mimi then pointed to her little back tooth,

which suddenly hurt whenever she chewed.

"Tilt your head high up to the sky

so that Mama can see better with the light."

Mama couldn't see anything either way her face was turned,

but because Mimi was in pain, Mama was still concerned.

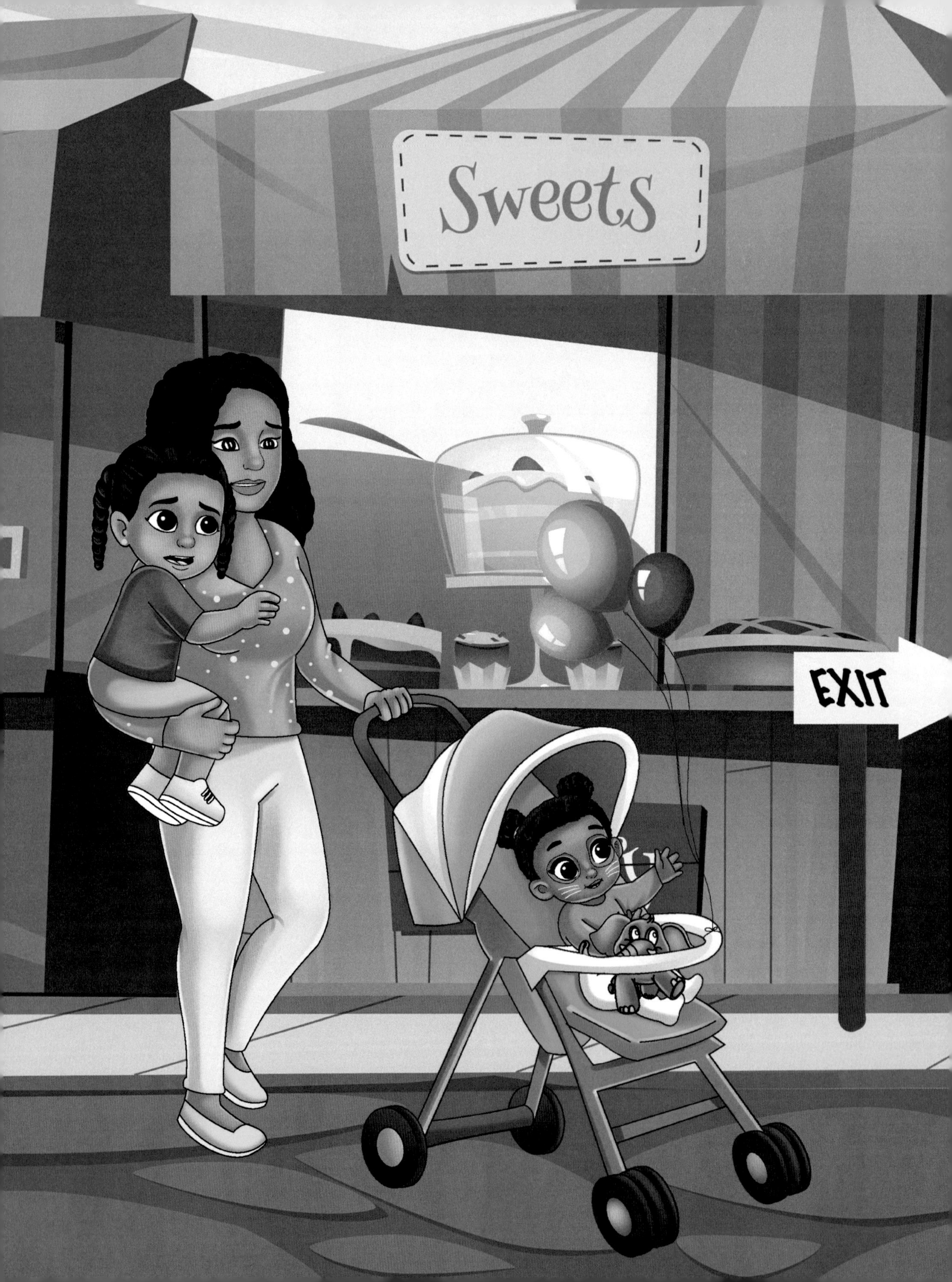
Sweets
EXIT

Mama scooped up the sad little girl,

who hid her face from the rest of the world.

Mimi rested her head on Mama's shoulders

as Mama pushed Baby-sis away in the stroller.

Stuffed animal prizes, county fair balloons,

a family portrait of the girls from a photo booth.

A sleepy, worn-out Baby-sis, Mimi clinging to her mother's hip.

She regretted the forbidden fruit which she'd unfortunately bit.

The blissful day had gone awry,

and to the fair, they waved goodbye.

Together, they added another happy memory to
their list

that would unexpectedly result in a trip to the dentist.

Mimi avoided sweets the next day,

and Mama gave her medicinc to make her
toothache go away.

After each meal that Mimi would eat,

she made sure to carefully brush her teeth.

It was only one day she'd have to get through

before her dental visit to check her tooth.

She watched cartoons and played with Baby-sis

and wondered what would happen at the dentist.

Before Mimi knew it, the day was done.

She said hello to the moon and goodbye to the sun.

As Mama read her a bedtime story,

Mimi drifted away into a night of glory.

The Sandman gathered up sand in a heap

to sprinkle into kids' eyes as they all fell asleep.

The next morning, the sun was ready to start his
new shift,

he let out a yawn, then the shining could begin.

Rays of shine crept into Mimi's blinds,

sprouting a light that opened her eyes.

Her body wasn't fully awake,

her joints were still stiff in a rigid state.

Bit by bit they loosened up,

like the Tin Man whose arms

seemed to be stuck.

Shoulders, elbows, knees, then toes.

Mimi's feet were up and ready to go.

She tip-toed her way around all of her toys,

then down the hallway, following a noise.

She saw a hot bowl of oatmeal, her favorite dish,

and Mama was feeding Baby-sis.

"Good morning, Mimi, how did you sleep?

Are you ready for the dentist to check your teeth?"

Mimi gave two thumbs up,

one for the oatmeal and the other for good luck.

With a smiley face of banana slices and raisins,

Mimi's oatmeal turned into an edible sensation.

Mimi's belly was full after she ate.

It was time to get dressed; she couldn't be late!

A cute little romper that Mama laid out

had a matching pair of sandals with a fuzzy
waist pouch.

Dressed, spiffy, and ready to go,

now it was time to make her teeth glow.

Mimi stood on a stepping stool

as Mama organized her teeth-cleaning tools.

Sparkly toothpaste, a couple of flossers,

a princess toothbrush, and a cup filled with water.

Mimi used a timer, which she thought was fun!

She would brush for two minutes, then she would
be done.

She rinsed and flossed, then it was time to leave

to go to the dentist and get some relief.

Mimi's teeth were sparkly clean,

and the girls were ready to hit the scene.

Through the hallway, down the elevator shaft,

across the lobby, onto Long Beach Ave.

Mama and the girls were greeted at the start of
their day

by the neighboring kids on the balcony who waved.

Past the colorful Impatiens that had recently
bloomed

and the taxi driver's honk that made a cat miss
his doom.

Across Brooklyn Avenue they strode,

to a fountain of water that beautifully flowed.

A cascading flow embellished the sign

for Doctor Jason's office, which looked so divine.

Dr. Jason was the best dentist in town

who took care of every child around.

His father was Mama's dentist when she was a kid,

but since then, the office had changed quite a bit.

Old Ms. Betty, the front desk lady, greeted them
with a smile

and recognized Mama when she and the girls arrived.

Beautiful artwork covered the walls

from Dr. Jason's patients who loved to draw.

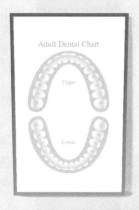

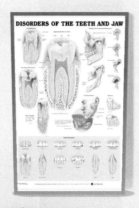

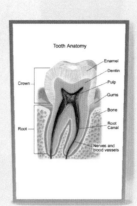

The waiting room was full of things to play with
and learn.

Kids built block towers while they waited their turn.

A bead maze was there to occupy the little ones,

and Baby-sis thought its colors and turns were fun.

"Hello, Mimi, it's good to see you, but not on these terms.

Mama tells me you have a concern.

Can you point to which tooth is troubling you?

We'll fix it right up; it'll be good as new."

Mimi pointed to the lower right with a pout,

where one tooth looked odd and really stood out.

"A-ha! Mimi! There appears to be

a peephole inside one of your teeth.

Let's have Ms. Suzy take an x-ray,

and then we'll see what the best treatment would be today."

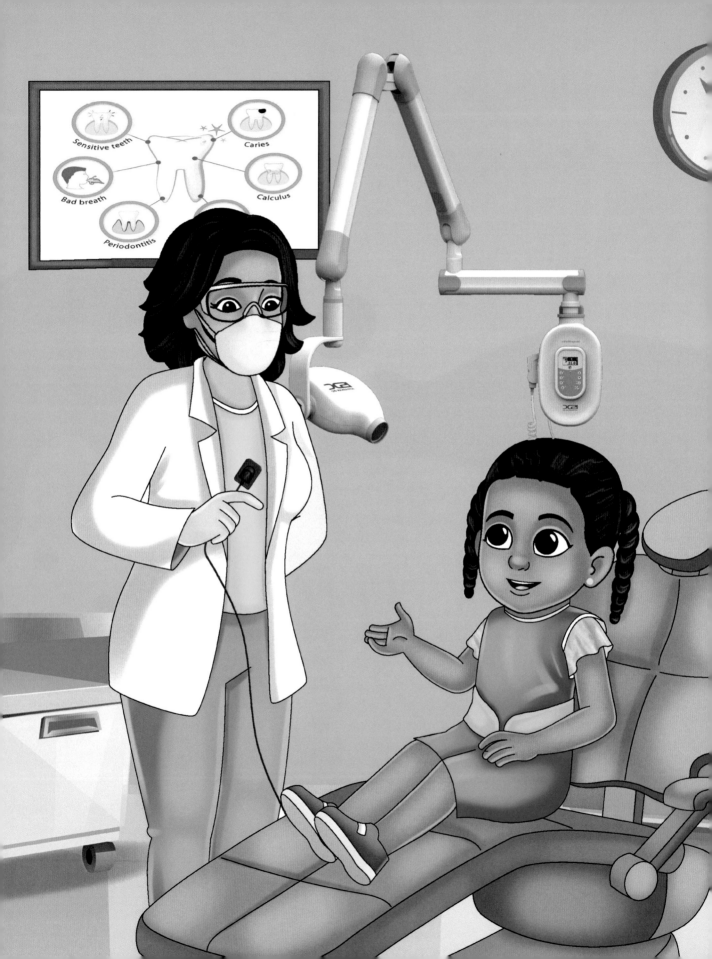

Ms. Suzy got a superhero vest

and carefully placed it on Mimi's chest.

Everyone else cleared the room

so they wouldn't get zapped by the "zap-a-roo."

"This is my cookie that you'll bite on,

attached to the sensor that touches your tongue.

Imagine yourself dancing in the rain.

I promise that you won't feel any pain.

I'll push a button to capture the image.

Once the *beep* stops, then you'll be finished."

Ms. Suzy lined up the x-ray machine

so it aligned perfectly with Mimi's teeth.

The cookie was placed, and Mimi bit down,

Ms. Suzy pushed the button, and no one *drowned*.

"Yay! You did it. The image looks great.

You'll feel better in no time at this rate."

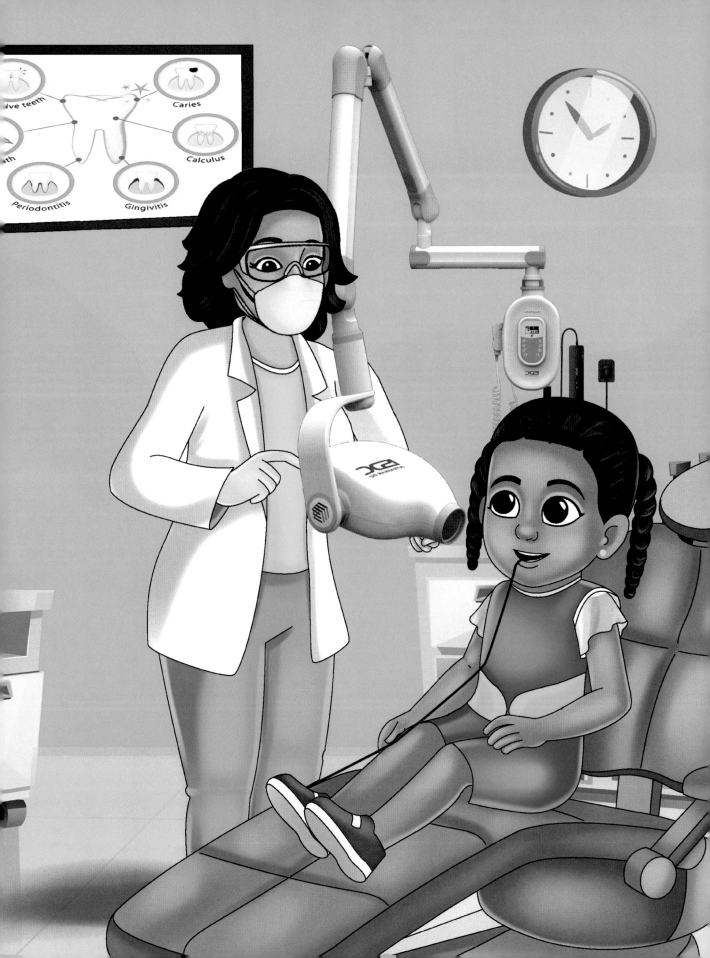

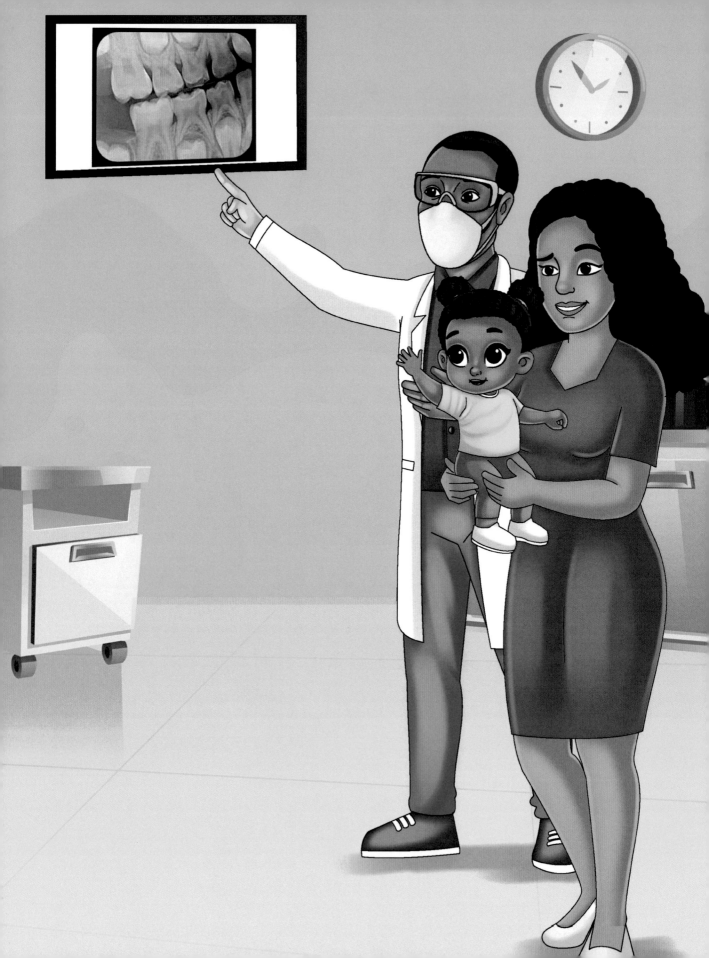

Mama and Dr. Jason returned to the room.

They all looked at the image as he examined her tooth.

"Good news, bad news," she heard the doctor say.

"One of your primary teeth has decay.

But because you were smart and came in so soon,

none of the decay has spread to another tooth.

Not to worry. I'll fix it right up.

We'll remove the sugar bugs and patch the tooth up."

Mimi was a little nervous and anxious inside,

for this was the first cavity she had in her life.

Ms. Suzy began to prepare her tools

and turned on the TV which played cartoons.

Over Mimi's chest, a patient bib was draped,

then she got a pair of safety glasses to protect her face.

Dr. Jason tapped on her tooth

and asked if she felt anything from his tapping tool.

"The first thing we'll do is put your tooth to sleep.

I'll place a little strawberry gel inside your cheek."

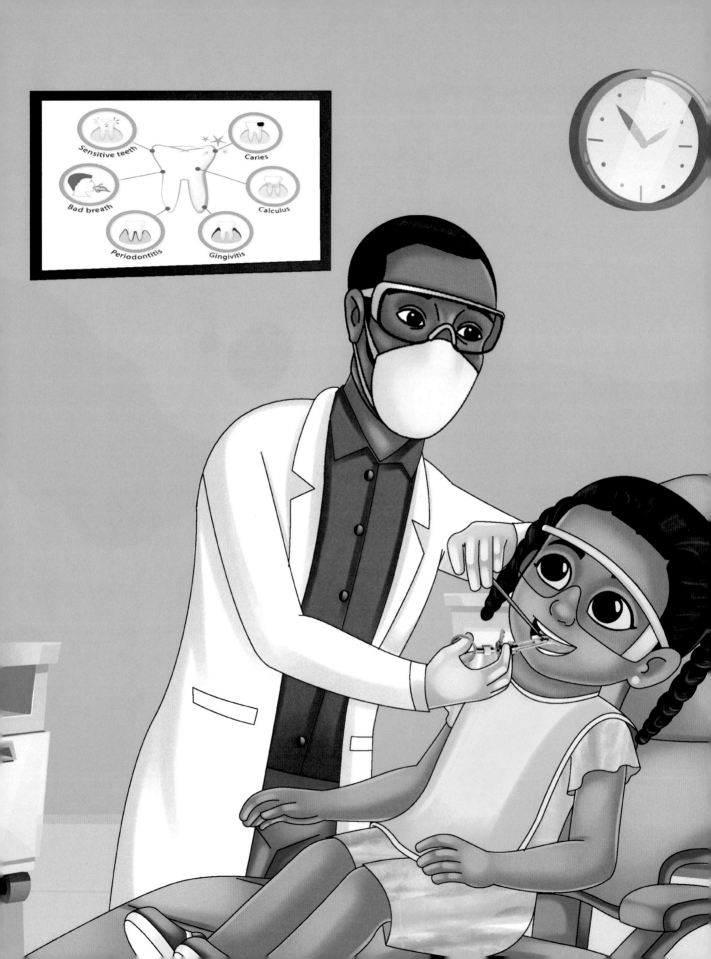

After a minute, he rinsed off the gel,

and Mr. Thirsty vacuumed the water as well.

"We'll give the tooth some *sleepy juice*

so he can rest as we make him brand new.

I'll count to four, then you'll feel a small pinch,

then I'll sit you up so you can rinse."

It was like a mosquito bite had pricked her gums

and within a few seconds, she began to feel numb.

When Mimi's tooth was finally asleep,

Dr. Jason checked to see if it was ready to treat.

He used Mr. Whistle to remove the decay.

The foot pedal rhythm made him whistle away.

It even made the water sprinkler spray

as Ms. Suzy suctioned the cloudy mist away.

Dr. Jason then changed the tune to a
low-pitched sound,

using Mr. Bumpy to smooth things down.

"You're doing great, Mimi," the dentist said

as she watched the TV above her head.

"All the *sugar bugs* have now been removed,

so I'll place a jewelry ring around your tooth.

This will hold the playdough in its place,

and the wooden sailboat will keep if from
floating away."

Ms. Suzy handed him a wooden triangle.

He placed it between the teeth as a wedged ensemble.

He painted the inside of Mimi's tooth blue

with a little gel that would dry her tooth.

He then began to shower off the gel with care,

and then he sprayed it with a burst of air.

He placed a pillow beside her tongue as she began
to drool

to soak up saliva that had started to pool.

He painted the tooth again with a *magic* bond

so the playdough would fuse to her tooth and
become one.

He used a special shaping tool

to redesign the original shape of her tooth.

Ms. Suzy dried it with a shiny blue light,

and it began to harden just right.

The wooden sailboat was first removed,

followed by the jewelry ring around her tooth.

Mimi was instructed to close her mouth

to give it a rest from being spread out.

"Good job, Mimi," the dentist said. "Let's check your bite.

I want to make sure that it's alright.

On this blue paper, you'll tap up and down,

chew side to side, and grind all around."

Mimi did as she was instructed,

then Dr. Jason checked her new tooth structure.

She slid her teeth and tapped up and down,

and when Dr. Jason checked, no blue marks were found.

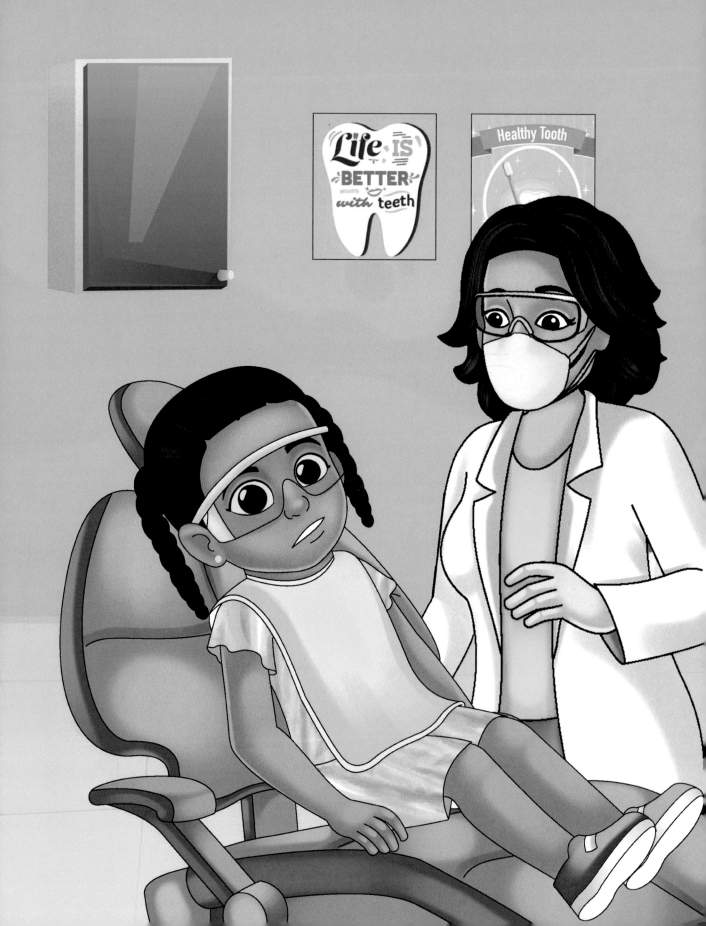

He pointed to one side of Mimi's face

to make sure everything was in the right place.

"Are your teeth touching together, would you say?

Or does it feel like something may be in the way?"

From what Mimi could feel, she felt sure

that her teeth were touching the same as before.

Mimi tried to smile, but one side was droopy,

and her lips and cheeks were slightly loopy.

"For a couple of hours, your tooth will be asleep.

Be sure not to eat; you could bite the inside of your cheek.

Brush twice a day and use your flossers," he said,

"and here's a special vitamin rinse to swish with before bed."

Try to avoid sticky snacks and gummy foods.

Make healthy choices, like vegetables and fruit.

Your Mama can help you accomplish these things

by helping you choose healthy but tasty things."

Mama gave two thumbs up.

Mimi did a great job, and she was so tough.

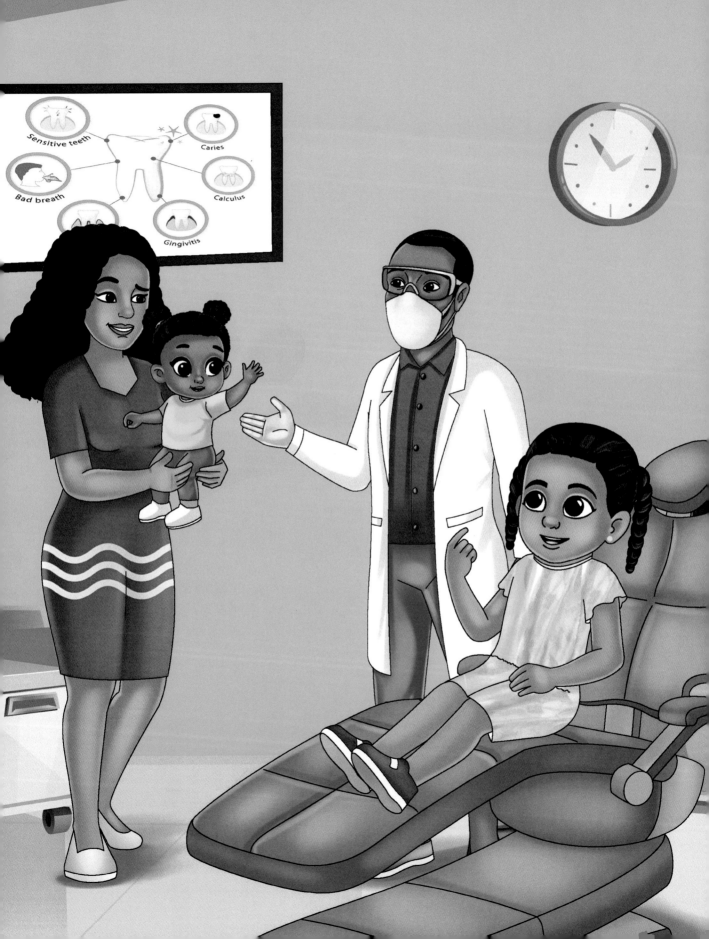

Ms. Suzy helped Mimi get all cleaned up,

then she picked from a treasure box with lots of cool stuff.

She picked a prize, a funny sticker,

and got a new toothbrush with her favorite character.

Baby-sis smiled at Ms. Suzy,

who handed her a ball that was so squishy.

Mimi was finished, and it was time to go,

then *old* Ms. Betty gave her a balloon for the road.

Mimi thanked Ms. Betty for the balloon.

Ms. Betty said, "You're so sweet! See you soon!"

Later on that afternoon, Mimi's tooth was fully awake.

The only thing she could drink was a yogurt shake.

Her tooth felt better, she was no longer in pain,

and she smiled brightly as she took on the day.

As a special thank you for fixing her tooth,

Mimi drew Dr. Jason a picture of all the animals at the petting zoo.

The very next day, she and Mama stopped by

to drop off her picture and to say hi.

Her picture had become a part,

of Dr. Jason's collection of his patient's art.

Old Ms. Betty added it to the wall with care,

and it blended in perfectly as though it belonged there.

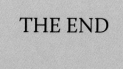

THE END

SING ALONG SONG

This is the way we brush our teeth, we do it every day.

We brush them in the morning, and when we go to bed.

We make sure that we floss them too, to keep away decay.

Swish, swish, swish.

This is our last defense.

To keep away the sugar bugs that bathe our teeth all day, yay!

DON'T MISS THE OTHER TITLES
WRITTEN BY THE AUTHOR

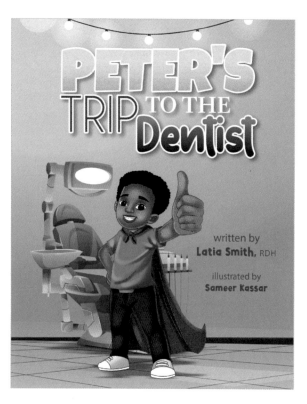

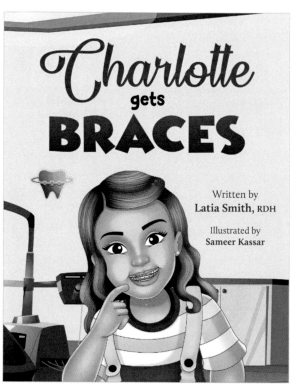

Please leave a review on Amazon and Goodreads.
Find Latia Smith, RDH on Facebook.

ABOUT THE AUTHOR

Latia Smith, author of *Peter's Trip to the Dentist* and *Charlotte Gets Braces*, continues to captivate the world of pediatric dentistry. The UNC Chapel Hill dental hygiene graduate developed her passion for writing children's dental books to create common scenarios that occur at the dentist. She brings to life a fun-filled atmosphere where comfort is provided by the dentist and staff in an environment created to meet children's needs. Her books educate readers and help build confidence in children to receive dental treatment.

Latia continues her role as a dental hygiene clinician, providing preventative oral hygiene care to patients. She advocates for oral health by educating her community with oral hygiene instructions, nutritional counseling, and ways to prevent oral disease. When she is not indulging in dentistry and creative writing, she enjoys spending time with family, traveling, and exploring new hobbies.

Made in the USA
Monee, IL
27 October 2023

45224765R00050